W9-ANH-943

JUNKYARD DOG

JUNKYARD DOG

by Sandi Barrett Ruch

illustrated by Marjory Wunsch

Orchard Books

New York

Orchard Books
A division of Franklin Watts, Inc.
387 Park Avenue South
New York, NY 10016

Manufactured in the United States of America
Book design by Martha Rago

10 9 8 7 6 5 4 3 2 1

The text of this book is set in 14 pt. Meridien.
The illustrations are ink and charcoal.

Library of Congress Cataloging-in-Publication Data
Ruch, Sandi Barrett.
    Junkyard dog / by Sandi Barrett Ruch ; illustrated by
Marjory Wunsch.
    p. cm.
    Summary: Follows the exciting adventures of Toad and mean old
Slobber, the junkyard dog, as they form an unlikely friendship
and find a place to call home.
    ISBN 0-531-05842-5. — ISBN 0-531-08442-6 (lib. bdg.)
    [1. Dogs—Fiction. 2. Toads—Fiction. 3. Friendship—
Fiction.] I. Wunsch, Marjory, ill. II. Title.
PZ7.R83145JU 1990
[Fic]—dc20   89-35652
                                                            CIP
                                                             AC

To my Pop, who brought me toads—
and beetles and bugs. And my husband Jim—
who believed I could write about all of them.
S.B.R.

THE JUNKMAN had a new dog. He was a massive dog, broad shouldered and square muzzled, with saliva dripping from his mouth. More like a wolf, Toad thought as he watched the dog leap about, growling and barking, jerking at the chain Zlotnick held tightly in his two hands.

The dog's grizzled black coat was tattered and unkempt, hanging in ropy tangles under his belly and down his heavy legs. Toad could make out close-set yellow eyes under shaggy brows and black lips curled back from dirty yellow teeth.

"He's so mean and ugly, only a junkman would have him," Toad said to himself, as he sat and watched from the mouth of his burrow under an old and rusting stove.

Zlotnick hurried to chain the new dog to the fence at the back of the junkyard. He filled an old bucket with water from the faucet and put it within the dog's reach. Then he found an old piece of cardboard and dragged it over to the fence. "There. You can sleep on that during the day."

The dog watched unblinkingly, his feet braced wide apart and his head lowered, ready for whatever might come next.

Zlotnick frowned at the dog for a minute. Then, with a hitch of his overalls, he went to rummage through a pile of lumber to find a large sheet of plywood.

"It's not much shelter, but you'll have shade during the day. You won't need anything at night," he muttered, propping the plywood up against the fence. "Night's when you'll be guarding this place, not sleeping all snug and cozy. My dogs work all night. That is, they do if they expect to stay."

When he was done, he stood back with his fists on his hips. "I got no food to waste on some worthless, lazy mutt that's going to let somebody break in here at night and steal me blind. I need the meanest, orneriest, fight-ingest dog I can get. If you're not mean enough, then out you go."

The dog growled—a deep rumbling sound that seemed to shake the ground under Zlotnick's feet.

Zlotnick stepped back quickly. "That's right, you keep that up and you just might stay," he said, nodding his head up and down. "But I'm not about to holler some fancy name like 'Maximillian' at an ugly dog like you." He chewed his lower lip and studied the dog. "Nope, you're Slobber now. . . . Yup, Slobber dog, that'll do just fine."

And hitching up his patched and faded overalls again, Zlotnick turned and hurried down the lane between the piles of junk to the truck, where his children were waiting.

All that day, Toad could hear the chain rattling against the fence as the dog tried to get comfortable on the shabby piece of cardboard. More than once Toad heard him bark savagely and lunge against the end of his chain when one of Zlotnick's customers dared to come too close.

There had always been guard dogs in Zlotnick's junkyard—huge shaggy beasts, their hair matted and dirty. They spent their days chained to the back fence. And if anyone did happen to come near them they would usually growl and show their teeth. But none of them had been exactly right—and one after another they had been sold or given away.

Now the junkman had a new dog. Toad wondered how long this one would last before it too was loaded into Zlotnick's truck and driven away, never to be seen again.

When the sun began to set and the last customer had found what he wanted, Zlotnick led his five children out of the front gate and put them into his truck.

"You be good, now. Papa will be right back," he said. Then, shutting the gate behind him, he went back inside the junkyard and turned his new dog loose.

I hope Zlotnick knows what he's doing, Toad thought

as the dog raced away, barking at imaginary thieves that lurked beyond the high wire fence surrounding the yard.

"Good dog, good dog, good dog," Zlotnick said over and over again, somewhat nervously. He hurried back through the front gate and locked it securely. Then after rattling it once, he climbed into his truck and drove away.

The dog was watching him, with his legs braced and his nose up to catch the scent.

As the truck disappeared around the corner, the dog put his head down and began to patrol. Around and around he went inside the fence. The sun sank lower and lower in the west and was gone.

One bright streetlight shone over the front gate, but in the junkyard there was only blackness.

TOAD WAS HUNGRY. Zlotnick had gone, and the sun had slipped below the mountaintops. It was time for him to leave the safety of his burrow and hunt the fat bugs and slimy pink worms that lived in the junkyard.

Deep within the darkest, dampest corner of his burrow, he hummed to himself:

Beetles and bugs
and crickets and slugs.
All of my dinner is lurking out there.

Robber flies bold
and cockroaches old
tremble and hide when I creep from my lair.

Toad knew that Zlotnick's junkyard was the very best place in the whole world to live. Everything he loved to eat lurked somewhere, every sort of beetle and bug, spider and worm, every slippery, slithery, slimy creature imaginable, and Toad's mouth watered as he considered them. Six-legged, eight-legged, a thousand-legged—it made no difference to him. None could escape. He would hunt them down and gobble them up.

Toad wiggled with anticipation. His eyes gleamed, and the gold in them became fiery flames. They were the eyes of a fierce and fearsome hunter.

Toad hopped past the chipped and rusty white bathtub, took a deep breath and continued around some wooden boxes of empty canning jars, turned left at the coils of black plastic pipe, and then decided he'd had enough hopping. His landings were becoming a bit sloppy, and he was breathing hard.

He was perfectly capable of hopping—of springing up into the air, his legs outstretched and ready to catch him when he landed. But he always came down with a plop like a swollen water balloon. Toad hated to plop. Not only was it embarrassing, it was uncomfortable, especially after a big dinner. But hops were faster, and when he was hungry, he hopped. Tonight he was very hungry indeed.

He often liked to find a quiet place and let his dinner

come to him. In front of the great pile of rotting magazines was the very best place of all. Shiny pink worms
and spiny silverfish and an occasional soft bug would
creep out of the rotting pages of *Jack and Jill* or *The
Saturday Evening Post*.

Crawling past the row of rusting washing machines,
Toad could see the jumbled piles of old magazines by
the pale yellow light of the half moon hanging low on
the horizon. The magazines were so rotten he could smell
them long before he reached them, and for years he had

worried that Zlotnick might haul them to the garbage dump. But Zlotnick was very slow about things like that. "Never know when something might have a buyer," he said one day, giving an old bathtub with a large hole in it a well-aimed kick.

Toad's mouth watered with anticipation as he squatted down in the dirt next to a rotting mound of *Life* magazines. His eyes narrowed until they were mere slits, and he became just another lump of dried mud. The beetles and bugs would never know he was there. They would come mincing out on their dainty legs, and in a flash, Toad would catch them on his sticky pink tongue. And then he'd eat them up, every last bit. Toad quivered with excitement.

"Munch them and crunch them," he hummed.

Suddenly a paw shot out from behind the magazines, pinning Toad to the ground. He gasped and closed his eyes. He should have known the dog would see him. Zlotnick's new dog would be especially on guard his first night.

Toad dared to open one eye. But the dog was behind him, and he could see nothing but a jagged toenail. He tried to compose himself. The dog might hurt him without meaning to. Then again, he might mean to.

WHAT NEXT? Toad wondered, trying to breathe under the weight of the dog's paw.

They both jumped when the sound came. A horn honked and a shiny yellow car rolled to a stop beneath the streetlight in front of the junkyard.

"Hey, Milo! You in there?" a voice shouted. The car door slammed and Toad heard the rapid click of footsteps on the sidewalk.

The paw was suddenly gone. Toad was free as the dog raced through the shadows toward the figure standing by the front gate.

"Hey, Zlotnick!" the man called again. "Found something for you. Not a dent in it! Worth at least five, maybe six bucks!"

Straining to see, Toad could just make out the dark mustache and sharp features of Zlotnick's friend Hotch Thorndyke. He was standing under the streetlamp, and its light reflected off a shiny hubcap he held in his hand. Toad heard the front gate rattle.

"Come on Milo! *Buy and sell* your sign says. I got something to sell. Come on, open up! I need the money real bad tonight."

The dog had stopped his headlong rush and was creeping, belly low to the ground, toward the front gate. He'd become a leopard, black on black, slinking through the night toward his unwary prey.

The dog halted just outside the circle of light and waited. His muscles were poised to spring.

"Hey, Milo, come on, open up!" The gate rattled again.

Like some great savage beast, the dog leapt at the man, an explosion of black, snarling fury and violence that crashed against the gate and hurled the startled man out into the street.

"Down boy, down! Get down!" Hotch yelped as he whirled around and ran to his car.

The engine sputtered and finally roared to life. With a squeal of tires, the yellow car was gone. Hurrying back to the safety of his burrow Toad could still hear the deep rumble of the dog's growl as he paced back and forth by the front gate.

It wasn't until he'd backed down into the deepest, darkest corner of his hole that Toad remembered he hadn't had anything to eat. He was very, very hungry. This is really too much, he thought, listening to his stomach growl and trying to forget the "beetles and bugs and crickets and slugs." All of his dinner was waiting out there. But so was the new dog.

Toad had never been sure what the junkyard dogs would do when he first met them. Usually there was just a curious sniff, and after that, he and the dog would ignore each other. Toad had certainly never been stepped on before.

He crouched down and tucked in his toes. No, after an experience like that, he would make sure that he and this new dog never met again. If he had to, he would wait until the very blackest part of the night, when the owls had finished flying and even the bats had disappeared into the darkest corners of the earth. Then, he was sure, the new dog would be curled up and asleep on some old mattress, and it would be safe for Toad to go hunting. He would wait.

Three times that night, Toad ventured out into the lane. Three times he saw the dog moving in the shadows, and each time Toad scuttled back into the dark recesses of his burrow.

When he saw the first fingers of light reach up into the eastern sky, Toad knew he would have nothing to eat that night.

THE NEXT MORNING, Toad lay in the deepest corner of his burrow and listened to his stomach rumble. He was very hungry, but after last night's narrow escape, he was glad to be back safe and snug under the stove.

Toad loved that stove. Under it, he was safe from all the terrible things that could happen to toads who lived outside Zlotnick's junkyard. When he was just a slim young toad, still with the memory of a tadpole tail, he had lived under a rock in the middle of a grassy field. The only frightening thing that ever happened was seeing a garter snake slither soundlessly past the mouth of his burrow.

But one spring day a steel-bladed harrow had come slicing through his field, overturned his rock, and destroyed his home. A gang of small boys had caught him as he fled for his life and passed him from hand to hand, laughing and poking and hurting. Toad's worst nightmares were filled with warm hands and jabbing fingers.

That night he had crept out of the field and under the fence into Zlotnick's junkyard. And while thunder crashed about him and lightning blazed across the sky, he had hurriedly dug a short and dangerous burrow under an overturned table. He'd moved again the next night, and a good thing too—before Zlotnick set the table back up on its three wobbly legs.

Toad dug his second burrow under a moldy rug that was home to a quarrelsome family of mice, but their constant squabbling finally drove him out, grumbling and snappish. He had to find a better place, someplace safe, someplace permanent.

After a long night of searching, he finally settled on the old stove, and under it he dug his third and last burrow. He was sure no one would ever notice it. But even if they did, it was just a small, dark hole, nothing unusual in Zlotnick's junkyard. Although if anyone looked very closely, and if the light was just right, and if Toad's great round eyes with their golden flecks were open, they just might see him hiding there, waiting for night to fall.

But no one had ever looked. The most that ever happened was an occasional poke under the stove with a sharp stick by one of the Zlotnick children. Toad didn't like to remember those attacks. He had decided that with the next rain, after the ground got very, very soft, he would put a sharp, right-handed bend in his burrow, beyond which he could retreat if any danger arose. But that would have to wait. The ground was dry and hard as a rock right now.

During the day, Toad would often crawl to the mouth of his burrow and watch all the things that went on in the junkyard. He couldn't see every part of it, of course. Half the junkyard was behind the old stove, but that half was the uninteresting part, full of old tires and rusty pipes.

In the front of the junkyard, where customers came and went, and where Zlotnick and the children spent their days—that was the interesting part. Right now, Toad could see Zlotnick, in blue dungarees and a pair of red suspenders, sitting in his chair under the awning of his shed. He was waiting for customers and watching his children play.

Crystal was the oldest, probably nine years old, Toad figured, counting on his toes. She was named for her mother, who'd been dead almost a year. Toad remembered Mrs. Zlotnick—a small, smiling woman who had fussed about the junkyard like the sparrows that flitted

through the wire fence collecting chair stuffing to line their nests.

Next was Frieda, a year younger, a pale, thin girl, with her nose always buried in a book. She never shouted or raced around the junkyard with the other children, tipping things over and scattering the sparrows. And she was certainly no match for the rowdy Crystal, who always bullied her.

After that, there was six-year-old Pearlie, who was like another Crystal with a head of thick yellow curls. Something of a brat, Toad thought. She was the one with the stick who went around the junkyard poking at things until her father got fed up and took it away from her. Toad had to keep a close eye on Pearlie.

Huey was next, the only boy, a chubby, red-cheeked four-year-old terror. Crystal loved him and mothered him, and it was her job to keep him out of trouble. But Huey didn't want to stay out of trouble. He would wait until Crystal's back was turned and off he'd go, scampering across the junkyard, searching for a new, exciting place to hide.

"Huey? Huey, where are you?" Crystal would call. Running up and down the lanes among the junk, she would search the wooden barrels and rusting bathtubs to see if there was a little boy giggling and hiding inside them. There were wooden boxes and round, green washtubs to climb inside, piles of lumber and rotting mattresses to squat behind. The junkyard was a wonderland of mysteriously dark and horribly smelly places where a little boy could hide, and Crystal had to search all of them.

When she found him, she would drag him out and pinch him so hard that his giggles would turn to howls. She would scold him and tell him never to do that again. But he always did.

The last of Zlotnick's children was Melba, just two years old. Melba thought that Huey, when he wasn't pulling one of her red pigtails or pinching her through the bars of her playpen, was the most wonderful person in the world. Today she was in her playpen pounding on a copper washtub with a spoon and singing a *la la la* song to all of her family.

Frieda and Pearlie and Huey were sitting on the ground in a row in front of Crystal. "Now, don't any of you go near Papa's new dog," she was telling them, looking especially hard at Huey. "He's mean and he might bite you."

Across the yard, the dog heard her voice and growled, a deep-throated rumble like the threat of distant thunder.

"You hear your sister? You do like she says," Zlotnick called from the shed, where he had gone to knock the dents out of a shiny almost-new hubcap. "You stay away from that Slobber dog. He's one mean animal, maybe the meanest I ever got. . . . You leave him alone, you hear?''

Crystal and Frieda and Pearlie and Huey and even Melba nodded their heads.

The new dog growled again.

So that afternoon, the Zlotnick children played in the front of the junkyard while Melba watched her older brother and sisters from her playpen. Toad watched them all until his eyelids became heavy, and he retreated again into the damp shadows of his burrow for a short nap.

"DOGGIE, NICE DOGGIE."

Doggie? What doggie was Huey talking about? Toad wondered, lifting an eyelid. Dog! Oh no! And, suddenly understanding Huey's words, he rushed to the mouth of his burrow. Before Toad had gone to take his nap, Huey and Pearlie had been jumping up and down on a pile of musty mattresses stacked behind the shed. Somehow Huey had crept away without Crystal seeing him, and now he was sitting in the dirt across the lane from the dog.

"Nice doggie. Want a cookie, doggie?" Huey asked, holding a chocolate cookie out to the dog.

The dog pricked up his ears.

"Good cookie," Huey assured him, and putting his fist back, he threw the cookie as hard as he could. The black dog ducked his head and flattened his torn ears as the cookie landed in the dirt halfway between them. The dog took a step forward, his eyes fastened on the little boy.

"Poor doggie," Huey said. "Can't get the cookie, can you doggie?"

Toad heard a low rumble in the dog's throat, and the air trembled with the sound. The dog's lips curled and his hackles rose.

Huey got up. "Funny doggie," he said. "Huey get the cookie for the doggie."

Toad held his breath. Huey's going to walk across the lane and pick it up, Toad thought. And when he does, he'll be close enough for the dog to bite him.

"Huey, don't," Crystal screamed, running down the lane toward him.

Huey picked up the cookie and turned slowly to look at Crystal, his lower lip sticking out. "The doggie wants my cookie," he explained.

"Huey!" Crystal screamed.

"Here, doggie," Huey said and walked to the dog, holding out the cookie.

Everything seemed to happen in the blink of Toad's eye.

As Crystal reached Huey and jerked him away from the crouching dog, the dog exploded in a sudden frenzy of barking, lunging against the chain that held him by the neck. Crystal pulled Huey up the lane toward the shed, holding him firmly by the arm.

"You keep away from that dog," she said, shaking her finger at her little brother. "He'll bite you."

"But he's a nice doggie," Huey argued, his lower lip even farther out.

"No, he's not. And he doesn't like little boys who throw rocks at him," she answered.

"But Crystal, it wasn't a rock, it was a cookie," Huey answered with a frown, shaking himself loose from her grasp.

"He's not supposed to eat cookies, he's supposed to be a mean junkyard dog. And if he isn't, Papa will have to get rid of him," Crystal explained, shooing Huey back to the pile of mattresses.

Toad took a very deep breath. The dog could have bitten Huey. But he hadn't, and Toad was glad. Zlotnick had a mean junkyard dog all right, but there were limits, and at least the dog seemed to know what they were.

At last the sun had crossed the sky and sunk behind the mountains. Dark shadows faded in the twilight as Zlotnick locked up his shed and put the children in his truck. With nervous mutterings he unchained his new

dog, and casting one or two anxious looks over his shoulder, he hurried out of the junkyard.

Toad dithered in the mouth of his burrow as the sound of Zlotnick's truck faded in the distance. What should he do? It was time for him to go hunting for his dinner. He hadn't eaten in two days, and he was so hungry his knees trembled. He had to find something to eat. But he was not going to leave the safety of his burrow if it meant being stepped on by the new dog again. Toad decided he would wait and watch and hope that the dog would finally tire of his new job.

But for the second time, when Zlotnick's truck came puffing around the corner in the morning, the dog was still at work. And all Toad had had for dinner was a crunchy gray wood louse that had foolishly stumbled into the mouth of his burrow.

"SLOBBER! HERE, SLOBBER! Come on, boy. Sit boy, sit Slobber. *Stay.*" Zlotnick stood outside the gate, his truck parked at the curb, with his children watching him through the open window.

"Be careful, Papa," Crystal called.

With teeth bared in a fierce but silent snarl, the dog padded across the open yard and watched Zlotnick as he unlocked the gate and slipped inside.

Toad had scooted as far out of his burrow as he thought was safe, stretching to the tips of his toes so he could see.

"Good Slobber. Good old boy," Zlotnick muttered,

standing with his back to the gate and a pan of dog food held out in front of him.

Head down, the dog stalked him. Zlotnick quickly set the pan down. "Good dog, good dog," he said again, slipping back through the gate and slamming it shut.

The dog stopped and stood over the food pan, his hackles up, watching the man.

At last the dog began to eat. When he licked up the last crumb, Zlotnick took a deep breath and inched slowly back inside the junkyard, his hand out until he was close enough to grab the dog's collar. Then with a great sigh, he led him to the back of the junkyard and chained him to the fence for the day.

The Zlotnick children played in the front of the yard under the watchful eyes of Crystal and their father. Even Huey seemed to be minding, and he only ran as far as the old bathtub. There he played happily with a three-wheeled truck until Crystal dragged him away for his lunch of a peanut-butter-and-jelly sandwich and a strawberry soda.

When he wasn't watching his children, Zlotnick would get up and yawn, stretching his arms wide. "Going to find a way to get rich today, no doubt about it," he'd say, turning to go inside the shed and work on a piece of junk he thought he might be able to repair. A lamp that needed a new cord, a toy wagon that needed a wheel, a chair that needed another leg—anything that might bring in a little more money.

Later, over the growling of his stomach, Toad heard the telephone ring.

Zlotnick came out of his shed and took down the receiver. " 'Lo?" he said.

"That you, Milo?"

Toad could hear the voice over the telephone clearly, even at that distance. It was old Mrs. Mauk from down the street.

Not waiting for his answer, she went on. "Sonny bought me a new dishwasher for my birthday—and a fridge, a nice big one. They're going to be delivered any minute now. You want my old ones? You come and get them now!" she shouted over the telephone.

Toad saw Zlotnick wince. Talking to Mrs. Mauk was a painful business when she didn't have her hearing aid on.

"They work?" he bellowed back, so loud the stove over Toad's head seemed to shake. But she'd already hung up.

Zlotnick loaded his children into the truck and banged the front gate shut, not bothering to unchain the dog. In a few minutes he was back with the stove and the refrigerator in his truck—and a big smile on his face.

Mrs. Mauk hadn't bothered to empty them out, so they traveled to the junkyard with a chipped teacup nodding lazily on the rack in the dishwasher and the remains of a head of lettuce and a withered carrot still in the bottom drawer of the refrigerator.

Zlotnick washed and dried the two appliances with an old rag and polished them until they shone. "Going to get rich today," he hummed as he polished.

"Yes, Papa," Frieda said, not looking up from the tattered book she was reading. And Huey, who was playing in the mud, clapped his hands.

When Zlotnick was done, he called all his children

around him and warned them never to touch the new dishwasher or the new refrigerator. "I don't want any dirty fingerprints or any scratches on that shiny enamel, you hear? So don't you kids touch them, not ever. You hear me?" he repeated, fixing them with a stern glare that made them all quiver. "You understand?" And when they all nodded, he shooed them away.

The new appliances were given a place of honor in the center of the junkyard, right behind the oak table with three legs. They were so lovely, gleaming there in the sunlight. They gave the yard class, and when Zlotnick sold them he would make a lot of money.

He'd had a few expensive things in the junkyard before—an old bathtub with claw feet that someone paid him twenty-five dollars for. And once he even got thirty dollars for an old treadle sewing machine. But nothing as exciting as this.

The refrigerator was quite old really, with a few dents in the door, but it did work. At least that's what Zlotnick wrote on the front of it in purple crayon: $65. WORKS GOOD.

Mrs. Mauk said the dishwasher leaked a little, so he wrote $25 on it.

They were certainly the two finest pieces of junk in the yard, the sort of things you'd expect to find in a secondhand store.

"Next there'll be new stoves and new washing

machines and tables with four legs," Toad lamented. "And then there'll be a proper store with proper floors and walls and a roof to keep out the rain. And a pest man to kill the beetles and bugs. And no place for a poor old toad."

While Zlotnick and his children were having lunch, Mr. Dewberry and his wife came and offered Zlotnick ten dollars for the dishwasher. After Zlotnick absolutely refused to take anything less than eleven dollars, they hauled it away in the back of their green pickup truck.

Now the refrigerator stood alone in gleaming, icy splendor in the center of the yard. Only a few customers showed any interest. They would walk around it a few times, tug at the door handle until it finally popped open, peer inside, and after a few minutes, wander off to look at something else.

TOAD HAD BEEN dreaming of fat green caterpillars when he slowly became aware of someone not very far away talking to the dog. It was Huey.

He's going to be gobbled up completely if he isn't careful, Toad thought, scurrying to the front of his burrow.

"And someday you can come home with us, and you can sleep with me in my bed," Huey was saying.

Toad held his breath. Huey was sitting beside the ugly black dog, an arm around his neck, feeding him crusts from his sandwich. "I'll throw balls for you to chase, and if you like, I will give you a bath," he added, petting the dog's rough coat. "But if you don't like to take baths, that's all right with me. I think baths are awful too."

Where was Crystal? Why wasn't she watching him? She was usually so careful about Huey.

Hardly believing his eyes, Toad saw the dog nibble bits of sandwich crust from Huey's fingers. What was the dog going to do when there was nothing left for him to eat?

"Huey! Where are you?"

At last, it was Crystal. She would stop what was happening. Toad could hear her bare feet slap the ground as she ran down the junkyard lane toward Huey. If only she gets to him in time, Toad worried. When the sandwich crusts are gone, the dog might eat Huey.

"No!" Crystal screamed.

The dog scrambled to his feet, peering at the running girl through hooded eyes.

Toad held his breath, afraid to watch, afraid not to. What would the dog do? Toad could see the taut muscles in the dog's shoulders quiver as he prepared to lunge at Crystal if she came too close. "No, don't," Toad whispered, hoping that the dog might hear.

Crystal stopped, her body rigid, and held out her arms. "Come over here, Huey," she ordered in a level voice. "Come slowly. Don't upset the dog."

Toad marveled at how calm her voice was.

Huey stood up and frowned at his sister, not sure that he understood why she wasn't angry. He brushed the dirt off the seat of his jeans and patted the dog on the head. " 'Bye," he said and went to Crystal.

When he was safely outside the reach of the dog, she grabbed him and shook him roughly by the shoulders. "I told you to stay away from that dog, didn't I? Didn't Papa? You're not supposed to pet him."

"But he's a nice dog," Huey answered, kicking at a dirt clod with his toe.

"No, he's not," Crystal said and dragged him toward the shed. "And if you don't be good, Papa is going to spank you."

That was close, Toad thought. What would the dog have done if Crystal hadn't come? Would he have bitten Huey? Toad didn't think Zlotnick would own a dog that would hurt his children. Then again, isn't a good junkyard dog supposed to be mean?

There was a sudden squeal of tires in the street in front of the junkyard. A horn honked, and a shiny yellow car rolled up to the curb and stopped. The car door slammed and Toad strained to see who it was.

"Hey, Milo, you there?" a man shouted, and Toad recognized the sharp features and black mustache of Hotch Thorndyke. It was the same man who had come to Toad's rescue the night the new dog found him outside of his burrow and stepped on him.

"Hey Milo, I been looking for you. I got something I know you'll want to buy," Hotch yelled as he came through the gate, waving a hubcap in the air. "*Gen-u-ine*, grade A, right off one of those zippy little foreign cars," Hotch said. "You'll be able to sell this one fast, and I don't want much for it. . . . Only a couple dollars," he added with a laugh.

Zlotnick shook his head. "Yeah, I'll just bet," he said with a snort. But he took the shiny hubcap that Hotch held out to him.

The two men disappeared inside Zlotnick's shed, and in the sudden silence, Toad could hear a deep and dangerous rumble from the dog's throat. It was a frightening sound, and Toad wondered if it would ever be safe for him to hunt beetles and bugs in the junkyard again.

THE JUNKYARD wasn't a busy place, but every day a few people came and went, buying and selling. Some were searching for undiscovered treasures they could fix up and resell. Some came just to look.

"Oh Steve, come see what I found!"

The nearby voice startled Toad, who had been deep in his hole planning his evening's hunt and the cautious route he would take to avoid the dog. The woman sounded young and excited.

"Come look," she called again.

"What is it, Amanda?" the man asked. Toad watched a pair of big feet in dusty blue-and-white sneakers pass the entrance of his burrow.

"It's an old stove, just like the one Mother has up at the cabin."

Steve grunted. "Okay, you're right. So?" He was obviously bored.

"Well, look." She sounded exasperated now. "Don't you see. The handle on the oven door isn't broken."

"No, but the oven sure is," Steve laughed.

"I know, silly." She was being patient. "But you know how Mother has been trying to get a new handle for hers, and there just aren't any."

"Of course not. That stove must have been made before the First World War. What your mother needs is a new stove."

"But she loves that old stove. Her grandmother used to bake gingerbread cookies on cold winter days. She says she only has to look at that old stove to smell cookies baking and remember Christmas on the farm. Oh Steve, let's buy this for her. Then she'll have all the parts she needs. It's only twenty-five dollars, and I'll bet he'll take less if we make an offer."

"I don't know, it looks awful rusty—and heavy," Steve answered. Toad could see his feet moving around. Toad's heart began to beat faster. They wouldn't really take his stove. They wouldn't destroy his home, not after all this time!

"Oh come on, Steve. This will be a wonderful present for Mother. Let's go make the junkman an offer."

The feet disappeared and it was quiet again, but any minute now they might come and take the stove, and they'd see poor Toad. What would they do when they saw him? Would they hurt him? Most people thought toads were ugly and awful.

Shaking with fear, Toad crawled to the front of his burrow and stuck his nose out. There was no one in sight. Perhaps he could make a dash for it and find some place to hide. But it was too bright, too exposed, and Toad knew he wasn't the dashing sort.

In the distance, he heard voices coming back toward him. Toad was so frightened he could hardly move. It wasn't until he saw Zlotnick's boots that he scooted back into his burrow as far as he could go.

"Well, I don't know. That's a fine old stove," he heard Zlotnick say.

"Hah," the man named Steve laughed. "It's rusty, and the oven door won't shut. We'll give you ten dollars for it. And no more."

"Well now, that's a real antique. I might take twenty dollars for it, but no less," Zlotnick countered.

"Forget it," Steve answered. "Who knows how much rust there is on the bottom where it's buried in the mud."

Toad trembled. "Oh, please don't sell my stove," he prayed. Ten dollars isn't enough. Zlotnick would never take ten dollars for something as wonderful as Toad's stove.

"Well," Zlotnick said, considering the offer. "How about fifteen?"

"Nope, that's my final offer. Ten dollars."

"Well," Zlotnick said again, and Toad held his breath. "Say 'no'—say 'no'—say 'no,' " he prayed.

"Sold," Zlotnick said with a sigh.

Poor Toad was terrified. Were they going to rip the roof off his home right now and find him huddled there? What would they do when they saw him? What would *he* do? Toad shivered. Oh, it was the end of everything.

"We'll be back Saturday with a truck to pick up the stove," Steve said.

The voices faded and were gone.

Toad stopped trembling and took a very deep breath and counted to ten. He let his breath out slowly. Saturday. That would give him enough time to move. All he had to do was find someplace in the junkyard where the ground wasn't too hard and dry, someplace safe where he could dig a new burrow.

THE NIGHT WAS dark, with no moon, and a dry wind from the south blew clouds of dirt through the junkyard. There was the hint of early autumn smoke in the air, a tangy smell of burning maple leaves.

Up and down the lanes Toad hopped, searching among the rows of junk for something solid, something heavy, under which he could dig his new home. But everywhere he looked the ground was dry and hard, much too hard to tunnel into. All he would be able to dig was a short and dangerous burrow.

He had abandoned all of his cautious plans. In fact, he had actually forgotten that there was a new dog in the junkyard. Toad's mind was on only one thing—finding someplace in the junkyard where he could dig a new burrow. Someplace safe, someplace where no one would ever disturb him again.

An old sofa, its red and yellow flowers like smudges of dirt in the faint light, was a possibility, but Zlotnick's children liked to bounce up and down on it, and he abandoned that idea.

An old television set tipped over on its side was another possibility, but a large black rat with pink eyes declared himself the rightful tenant, and Toad backed away.

Finally dawn came, catching Toad on the other side of the junkyard, beside the lumber pile. The long night was over, and he had to hurry home. Zlotnick would soon be unlocking the gate.

"One night already gone, and I haven't found a single possible place where I can dig my new burrow," Toad muttered as he turned to go home. The whole night had been a waste.

Where will I go and what will I do? he wondered. At least he had until Saturday. Tonight, after a long and restful nap under his stove, he told himself, he would find just the perfect place.

With a sudden pang, Toad realized how very hungry he was. Oh, it had been such a long time since he had had a good meal, and he tried not to think of the rose chafers and bagworms he had missed. He was sure he had shrunk to only half his normal size.

But the sun was rising, and most of the beetles and bugs in Zlotnick's junkyard were by now tucked away in some dark place, safe and snug where no hungry toad would ever be able to find them.

A woolly bear inched out from among the thistles, and Toad froze. The fuzzy caterpillar was hunting for someplace to spend the winter, but Toad didn't care. He cared only that the woolly bear had spent the summer getting fat on Zlotnick's weeds.

The caterpillar crawled closer, and with a lunge Toad had him. He closed his eyes and swallowed.

Woolly bear fuzz
Is no bother because
I munch them and crunch them and spit out the hair,

Toad hummed, trying to forget how wretched he felt.

But it was getting light, and he had to hurry home before Zlotnick and the children came and caught him out in the open.

"Leaving already?"

Toad looked wildly about. The new dog was sitting on the other side of the lumber pile, his ragged ears cocked, watching Toad with yellow eyes.

"We have already met, I believe," the dog said. "But unfortunately we were interrupted."

"Yes," Toad answered, remembering the heavy paw and the long toenails from their last meeting. Would the dog step on him a second time? Or would he decide to bite him? Toad flattened himself, digging his toes into the dirt, and closed his eyes. If the new dog did decide to bite him, he'd find out how bitter tasting Toad was and leave him alone forever. On the other hand, even a quick taste could mean the end of poor old Toad.

"MY NAME IS Maximillian, and I am the new junkyard dog." The dog announced this proudly, his head and ears up. "But you may call me Max," he added.

"Maximillian?" Toad asked and frowned, not sure he had heard correctly. But of course he had, and he remembered how Zlotnick had changed the dog's name that very first day.

The dog nodded. "I was given the name Maximillian when I was just a puppy, but it has been years since anyone has called me that. If you would call me Max, I would consider you my friend." The dog turned his head and growled softly, his eyes on the fence and the orange sun rising beyond it.

Toad stared at the dog's curled lips and dirty yellow teeth. It was no wonder that Zlotnick had called him Slobber. Toad had opened his mouth to answer when his ears suddenly caught a whisper of sound deep in the lumber pile. There was something in there, something a hungry toad might like to eat. But he mustn't move, mustn't scare it, mustn't even breathe.

After a few moments of silence, the dog turned back, his brow furrowed with concern. "I'm sorry I stepped on you the last time we met. I'm afraid I get a little excited sometimes. I didn't hurt you, did I?"

"No, no, of course not," Toad murmured, crouching down beside the lumber pile so that he resembled nothing more than a small, warty rock.

"This is a fine junkyard, as junkyards go," the dog went on. "I've lived in many that were much worse, where no one fed me or brought me fresh water. At least the junkman is kind to me and doesn't beat me with a stick."

A pair of wiry antennae appeared between the boards, testing the early morning air. The dog scratched his ear with one back paw, and his jingling collar sent the cockroach scuttling back into the depths of the lumber pile. Toad tried not to groan.

"Yes, this is a fine junkyard," the black dog continued, looking around. "I was worried at first. Not sure what the junkman expected of me. But I think I'm going to like it here.''

Toad stared at the ugly dog with astonishment. What kind of a dog was there under all that meanness and ugliness? he wondered, forgetting the cockroach for a moment.

"And you live underneath the old stove, I believe," the dog said, turning his head to look at Toad.

"Umph, yes, of course," Toad grumbled, remembering his troubles. "But only until Saturday. Zlotnick has sold my beautiful stove, and now I have to move. It's not fair, it's just not fair. I'll never find a better place to live," he fumed. "But on Saturday, the stove that I have lived under all of these years will be dragged away, while I barely escape with my life. Believe me, there's nothing worse than the horrible slipping, sliding sound of Zlotnick's sled coming to haul away a piece of junk, if you're hiding under it!" His heart was pounding, and he had to stop to take a deep breath.

"My goodness," the dog said, surprised by Toad's outburst. "This is a big junkyard. Surely you can dig a new hole anywhere you want."

He saw the look in Toad's eye and hurried on. "It's different for a dog like me. I've got no choice at all about where I live. Zlotnick wants a mean dog to guard his junk, so here I am, chained to a fence all day and sleeping

on a smelly old scrap of cardboard with only a piece of plywood to keep out the sun and the rain." He sighed deeply. "And that's how it will be for the rest of my life. I'll never have what I want."

"And just what do you want?" Toad asked, not feeling quite so fretful.

The dog stared down at him. "Do you really want to know?" he asked, his voice full of surprise. "Really?"

Toad nodded.

The two black antennae were back, waving in the early morning air. Toad's eyes narrowed to mere slits as he calculated the distance.

"I want a house, a real house," the dog said. "A house with a door, and walls to keep out the wind, and a roof to keep out the rain. And a nice soft carpet to lie on. And every now and then I'd like to have someone scratch me behind the ears and tell me how wonderful I am."

"You're about as likely to get a fancy house like that

as I am," said Toad. "And as for the rest of it, well, nobody loves a mean and ugly junkyard dog any more than they love an ugly old toad like me. We're not the lovable sort."

The dog lay down and put his head between his front paws, his nose only an inch or two from Toad. "I know," he said. "But sometimes it's very hard not to want a scratch behind the ear or a chocolate cookie."

"And besides," Toad added. "If you were the lovable sort, I'm sure that Zlotnick would get rid of you."

Toad remembered the other junkyard dogs. Some of them had let the children pet them and had licked their faces and chased the balls they threw. One had even let Crystal dress him in baby clothes and wheel him about in an old wicker perambulator. Toad also remembered the familiar scowl on Zlotnick's face, and the next day the dog would be gone.

"But this is a nice junkyard. I like living here," the dog said, sitting up on his haunches. "I don't want Zlotnick to get rid of me."

Toad shrugged, a toadish sort of shrug. "Then, Maximillian, you will have to go on being a mean junk-yard dog," he said.

The cockroach suddenly came scampering out from under the board, antennae back, apparently oblivious to its fate. Toad leapt, his mouth open wide. But the cockroach had been ready and wasn't where Toad expected it to be. His jaws snapped shut on empty air.

When Toad opened his eyes and looked around, the cockroach was gone. "I must go now," he said with a scowl. "The sun is up and they'll be coming soon." And with that, he scooted as fast as he could across the junkyard toward his stove.

"Good-bye," the dog said.

"Good-bye," Toad called back . . . "Max," he added, turning the corner past the new refrigerator. The dog had said that if he would call him Max, he would consider him a friend. Well, there was no reason he couldn't be Max's friend. They were two of a kind, weren't they?

Zlotnick was rattling the front gate as Toad slipped into his hole and settled himself for a day of sleeping. He was disturbed only once, when something banged the stove above him, but it was only a customer seeing if the oven door would shut. It wouldn't.

THAT NIGHT Zlotnick had been gone only an hour when Toad heard the old truck come rattling back down the street. Yes, it was Wednesday, Toad remembered, watching Zlotnick unlock the big front gate.

"Slobber! Here boy. Sit boy," he called as the dog bounded toward him, snapping and snarling.

Toad smiled. Great move, Maximillian. Show Zlotnick just how mean you can be.

Zlotnick backed toward the open gate and his voice got louder and angrier. "Doggone it, Slobber. You sit, you hear? Sit boy!" His voice was gruff but Toad heard fear in it. Serve him right if the dog wouldn't let him in. What a Wednesday night that would make.

Still growling, the dog finally sat.

"Stay!" Zlotnick ordered, cautiously approaching the big dog with the yellow teeth. Warily, he grabbed the dog's collar and led him to the back fence. There he chained him and hurried back to the shed.

A car drove up and two men got out. Toad recognized Duffy and Thorp. Duffy was short and fat with a lot of unruly red hair that shone in the streetlight. Thorp was a little taller and a lot skinnier, and the streetlight made his bald head gleam. They both greeted Zlotnick loudly and disappeared into the shed.

The next car to arrive was old and blue. It had a hole in its muffler and a cloud of smoke followed it down the street. The man that got out was smoking the stump of a cigar. Turk Malloy, the garbageman.

A few minutes later a shiny yellow car drove up and parked behind the first. Quite evil looking, Toad had always thought, watching the familiar figure of Hotch Thorndyke disappear into the shed.

For the next five hours the men sat in the shed and played cards. The game had been going on every Wednesday night for as long as Toad could remember. Always the same five men sitting on wooden boxes around a broken card table in Zlotnick's shed.

In the winter they used a wood stove to keep them warm, and in the summer they opened the windows and

turned on an old fan with a bent blade that rattled and clanged as it spun.

Always the same five men with the door tightly shut, but tonight the new dog was chained up, far away from the shed. He couldn't hear what was going on, couldn't see the men, and Toad was glad.

Crawling out of his burrow, Toad made his way to the back of the junkyard. As he approached Maximillian, he could see the yellow eyes of the dog gleaming in the reflected streetlight.

"What are they doing?" Maximillian asked, with his eyes on the distant shed.

"The men? Oh, they're playing cards. They do that every Wednesday night. You'll see."

"Oh?" The dog sounded interested.

"Consider it your night off," Toad said.

Pawing at the piece of cardboard Zlotnick had given him for a bed, Maximillian turned around three times and lay down.

"It must be nice to have friends like that, friends you can count on to be there, week after week," the dog said.

Toad laughed, a deep harrumphing sound from his fat belly. "Yes, Riley wanted them to be his friends too."

"Who's Riley?" the dog asked.

"He was a large, spotted dog with a mean eye, sharp teeth, and very bad breath. He barked a lot."

"But Zlotnick got rid of him?" the dog asked.

"He sure did, but personally I think what happened was more Zlotnick's fault than Riley's," Toad replied.

"*What* was Zlotnick's fault?"

"Well, it all happened because of that card game," Toad said, nodding toward the shed. A darkling beetle scurried past and Toad lunged at it but missed. He made a few practice lunges just in case another one happened by.

"How do you know?" the dog asked.

"Because I was there and I saw what happened. I was hiding under a pile of empty beer bottles—a great place, I might add, to catch fat flies."

The dog wrinkled his nose, but Toad ignored him and continued. "I'd been there since closing time and I'd forgotten that it was Wednesday. I was there when Zlotnick unlocked the door of the shed and came in. I had to wait until long after midnight before I could finally leave."

Toad remembered with ecstasy that warm night with the old fan *ting-ting-tinging* in the background. That had been his finest hunt; fat beer-laden flies buzzing inside the bottles, frantically trying to get out, falling right into Toad's waiting mouth.

"Just you and the five men?" Max asked.

"No, Riley was there too. Zlotnick had always let the watchdog sleep under the table while they played. He kept him close for protection, I think. Anyway, that night, after the other men had left, and before he locked up and went home, Zlotnick hid his money in a jar he kept buried in the dirt floor of the shed."

"Money?" the dog asked, surprised.

"That's right. All the money he'd won playing cards."

The memory of that recent night was fresh in Toad's mind; the smell of cigarette smoke, the clink as another beer bottle was added to the pile in the corner, and the buzz of drunken flies. Now and then Duffy would reach down to hand Riley a cracker or give him a friendly pat on the head and scratch behind the ears. They were all friends, all six of them.

"So then what happened?" Max asked.

"Well, Zlotnick went home, and I crawled out under the side of the shed and went back to my burrow."

"No, I mean to Riley."

"Oh," Toad said, blinking his eyes. The gold flecks in them glittered in the moonlight. "The next morning Zlotnick discovered that his junkyard had been broken into. Someone had cut the lock on the front gate and kicked in the door of his shed."

"But where was Riley?" Max asked.

"Oh, he was there but the money wasn't. The jar had been dug up and all the money was gone. It must have been an awful lot of money, the way Zlotnick yelled."

"But why didn't Riley do anything? Didn't he see what was happening?"

"Oh yes, and that's what infuriates Zlotnick. Whoever took that money was a good friend of Riley's."

"Then Zlotnick caught the thief?"

"Well, no, but he knows it was one of four people. And that is why you're out here in the junkyard, my friend. And why you're chained up a long way from the men in the shed. Away from someone who would like to feed you crackers and be your friend."

"My friend?"

"And Zlotnick's," Toad answered.

The dog sat up. "I know who stole Zlotnick's money. I'll bet it was Hotch Thorndyke, wasn't it? The first time I saw him, I knew he was a thief."

Toad harrumphed. "As I said before, you're better off out here chained to the fence, where you won't start trusting people. Because the one who came back later that night and stole all of Zlotnick's money was Duffy, Riley's special friend."

12

"WHAT IN HEAVEN'S NAME are you two girls up to?"

The booming voice startled Toad out of a nightmare in which he was being chased by an enormous cockroach wearing dusty blue-and-white sneakers.

Poking his nose out of his burrow, Toad recognized Zlotnick's sister, Lola Karpel, standing in front of the shed. Her arms were folded across her ample bosom and there was a frown on her face.

Crystal and Frieda were sitting in the dirt and Crystal was braiding late summer daisies into Frieda's long brown hair while Frieda thumbed through an old movie magazine.

Pearlie and Huey had hung a sheet of blue canvas over Melba's playpen and were hiding inside with her, peeking through a hole at their Auntie Lola.

"Get up out of that dirt!" Lola bellowed, stamping her foot. Crystal and Frieda jumped up, brushing the seats of their jeans.

"Milo!" Lola bellowed again, and Zlotnick's head appeared around the door of the shed.

"What do you want, Lola?" he grumbled.

"Do you see what these two girls are doing?"

"Sure, they're playing."

"They are playing in the dirt, Milo. You've gotten awful sloppy with these kids since they lost their mama."

"So they're playing in the dirt. What's wrong with that?" Zlotnick asked, coming out of the shed and slamming the door behind him.

"Do you know that school starts next week?" Lola answered, glaring at him.

"So?" Zlotnick asked.

"So, they're ready, are they? They've got all their new clothes?" Her voice was heavy with scorn.

Toad squirmed with excitement and stretched up onto the very tips of his toes to make sure he wouldn't miss a thing.

"Well, no, I guess not," Zlotnick mumbled and glared at his sister.

"Oh, I forgot. . . . Someone took all of your money, didn't they, Milo? Well, we can't let that stop us from shopping for school clothes, can we girls?" Lola asked and smiled.

"Oh Auntie Lola!" Crystal squealed. "New clothes. For me?" She ran to her aunt and threw her arms around her.

"Now stop that," their Auntie Lola ordered, waving her hands in the air.

"Oh, can I have a new dress, Auntie Lola, a new dress with a ruffled skirt? And lace on the collar? Can I Auntie Lola, can I?" Crystal pleaded.

Frieda was watching her papa, the forgotten daisies lying scattered at her feet.

Zlotnick considered his two little girls, his thumbs hooked under his suspenders, and he finally nodded his head—a short, abrupt nod.

Frieda ran to her Auntie Lola. "And me too, can I have a dress too? A yellow one?"

Lola Karpel smiled down at the two girls. "Of course you can, darlings," she answered. "One dress each."

"And new shoes!" Crystal shouted.

"Shiny shoes," Frieda added. "With straps."

There was a rustling from under the blue canvas and Huey poked his head out. "Me too," he bellowed.

Lola Karpel laughed. "You too, what?"

"Me too, shiny shoes," Huey answered, climbing out of the playpen.

"Me, me," Pearlie said, following behind him.

"Oh dear," Lola Karpel answered, looking at her brother. "I can manage two kids today, Milo, but only two."

Huey began to howl. "Me too, me too," he screamed.

Pearlie began to sniffle.

"Milo?" Lola Karpel said.

"The rest of you hush," Zlotnick growled.

Their Auntie Lola clapped her hands. "Be good, and when we come back, we'll bring you all a lollipop," she announced. "Doesn't that sound good?"

Huey and Pearlie nodded. Melba began to sing, "Lolly, lolly, lolly."

"But right now, Crystal and Frieda are coming with me."

It was the last word and Lola Karpel had it.

Zlotnick went back inside his shed and slammed the door. As Toad watched, Mrs. Karpel took the grinning Crystal with one hand and Frieda in the other and led them out of the junkyard to her waiting car.

Huey and Pearlie stood silently in front of the shed beside Melba's playpen and watched them go.

The last thing Toad heard, just before he dozed off, was the toot of Lola Karpel's horn as she drove away.

"HUEY?"

"*Hu———ey!*"

The voice startled Toad, who was deep in the bottom of his burrow trying unsuccessfully to think of another rhyme for "bees and fleas."

"Huey?" Pearlie called again, closer this time. She was standing in the lane in front of Toad's door.

"Huey!" Toad heard Zlotnick shout from somewhere behind the stove.

Well, I'm not surprised they can't find him, Toad thought. Crystal wasn't here to keep an eye on that little terror, so of course he's disappeared. Wait until she gets back. She'll find Huey. She knows all of his secret hiding places.

"Huey!" Zlotnick called again, louder this time, and Toad tiptoed to a spot just within the mouth of his burrow where he could safely see what was going on in the junkyard.

Outside, the late afternoon shadows stretched across the dusty ground, and the sun was a hazy orange slice on the western hills.

As Toad watched, Pearlie looked in the old washing machines while Zlotnick searched under the pile of dusty, rotten rugs. He pushed aside stacks of newspapers and magazines, turned over large sheets of plywood, and upended empty barrels. But Huey was nowhere to be found.

"Huey?" Pearlie cried into the failing afternoon light. "Huey, where are you?" she called again, wandering through the piles of junk.

Toad saw Lola Karpel's car arrive, and in a moment Crystal and Frieda ran through the front gate, their arms full of packages.

"Hey! Where is everybody?" Lola yelled, bustling in behind the two girls, her hands full of orange and yellow lollipops.

Zlotnick poked his head out from behind the shed where he'd been searching in the pile of mattresses. "It's Huey. He's disappeared. I went to answer the telephone and when I turned around, he was gone! We've been looking everywhere."

"Well, I can't say I'm surprised," Lola Karpel said. "Maybe Crystal can find him." Everyone nodded.

But even after Crystal had looked in all of the secret places she knew about and in all of the places everyone else had already searched twice, the little boy was still nowhere to be found.

"He's gone out the front gate and wandered down the street. I just know it!" Lola Karpel insisted, hovering near the shed.

But Zlotnick shook his head. "No, no, he's here somewhere. He's got to be. He was only out of my sight for a second."

Watching from under his stove, Toad wondered why Maximillian was jerking at his collar, standing on his hind feet and lunging forward, practically choking himself.

"Milo, he's not here, he's gone," his sister argued. "I'm going to take the rest of these kids and search the neighborhood. Somebody must have seen him."

Frowning, Zlotnick watched his sister, with a wide-eyed Melba in her arms, herd the three other children into her car. She slammed the door and Toad heard the locks click before she drove away, leaving Zlotnick standing alone in front of his junkyard.

Automatically, he locked the front gate and hung up

the *Closed* sign. Then, seeming to collect his wits, he stopped and looked about.

He's decided that Lola's right. Huey has wandered off, Toad thought as he watched him. He's going to get in his truck and go look for him too.

"Huey?" Zlotnick called again, still hoping to hear an answer from somewhere inside the junkyard. But no one answered him as he hurried down the lane toward the chained dog.

"Huey?" he called again, his voice pleading. Reaching the fence, he grabbed the dog's collar, and after a moment of struggling, he unsnapped the chain and loosened the dog.

With a great bound, the black dog leapt away across the yard to the gleaming white refrigerator standing in splendor on its wooden pallet.

Standing on his hind legs, Maximillian put his front paws against the door of Zlotnick's new refrigerator and began to bark.

"Doggone it, Slobber. Get your mangy hide away from there!" Zlotnick yelled.

The dog's barking became frantic and he pawed harder, both feet digging into the shiny white door.

"I said, *get!*" Zlotnick bellowed. He was angry now. He reached down and picked up a hoe. Its broken handle was only a jagged point.

"You get away from that, you lousy hound," he shouted, holding the hoe up in a menacing manner.

But the dog wouldn't stop. Not now, not while he had Zlotnick's attention.

Toad saw the soft rubber seal of the refrigerator door pull away as Maximillian ripped at it with his claws.

Zlotnick saw it too. "Stop it! Stop it! You're ruining it!" he screeched as he ran toward the dog.

But the dog wouldn't stop. One of his paws raked across the shining white enamel, leaving several long black gashes.

That was the last straw for Zlotnick, but the dog didn't seem to hear the man's shouts or feel the blow across his back from the broken handle of the hoe.

"Get away, you crazy hound. *Get!*" Zlotnick yelled, landing another blow across the dog's back before he grabbed his collar and jerked him away.

"You've ruined it!" Zlotnick groaned, running his fingers down the long scratches in the white enamel door.

Beside him, the dog barked loudly again and again at the shiny white refrigerator.

Once more, Zlotnick swung his hoe at the dog. "You shut up, you hear me. I've had it with you, you good-for-nothing, worthless mutt. This is your last day in my junkyard!"

Then Zlotnick suddenly froze. He'd heard a faint

whimpering from somewhere nearby. "Huey?" he called. "Huey, where are you?"

The dog put his nose to the door of the refrigerator and whined.

Zlotnick pushed him aside and grabbed the handle of the door. He jerked at it until at last it clicked open. Huey tumbled out onto the ground in front of him. His face was red and tear-streaked, and as Zlotnick gathered him into his arms the little boy burst into tears.

"Papa, Papa, Papa," he whimpered over and over as Zlotnick carried him to the shed, ignoring the ugly black dog that followed at his heels.

14

TOAD WAS STARTLED early the next morning by the sound of hammering.

"How's a poor old Toad to think," he complained as he poked his nose out of his burrow. After listening for a while, he realized that the noise was coming from behind the shed. Another one of Zlotnick's "get-rich-quick" projects, he guessed, and scooted back into the deepest corner of his burrow.

He was going to miss his old home. The walls were cool and smooth, polished and shiny from years of use. He thought of all the other familiar things he would miss—the sound of rain on the stove top, the way the wind whistled through the flue, the lingering smell of burned dinners. He didn't want to move, but he must. Tomorrow was Saturday. Tomorrow Zlotnick would come with his sled and haul the stove away.

Toad sighed. Where was he going to dig his new burrow? The idea of going back into the open field filled him with terror. The best hunting spots were inside Zlotnick's junkyard. No, he wouldn't leave. He would stay. But where?

And if he did find the right spot, how would he be able to dig with the ground as hard as this? In all the

years he had lived in Zlotnick's junkyard, he couldn't remember a summer when the ground had been so dry. Digging with all of his toes and all of his strength, he would never be able to make even the smallest hole. He would have to find someplace temporary, someplace not very safe at all, where he could hide until the rains came. And on top of that, today would be ruined by all the worrying he had to do and tonight he would have indigestion.

He heard a squeal outside. Huey was on the loose again, but this time Crystal was close behind him, both of them running down the lane between the piles of junk, both of them smeared with bright blue paint.

Crystal caught Huey just as he dove into the bathtub. Pulling him roughly, she led him back behind the shed where Zlotnick was still pounding away with his hammer.

Dark gray clouds were scudding across the sky and the wind began to pick up, tossing old newspapers around the junkyard. Dust and dirt eddied around Toad. He closed his eyes and wished the rain would come. Rain would soften the ground; rain would make it possible for him to dig a new burrow; rain would make the junkyard nice and muddy. And right now, he thought with a wiggle, he would enjoy a nice mud bath.

Once or twice during the day he heard the dog's chain

rattle as Maximillian tried to make himself comfortable on the old piece of cardboard under the plywood. Not much comfort, Toad thought, not if there's a storm coming. And he must be wondering when Zlotnick will be getting rid of him for ruining the fancy refrigerator that the garbageman had hauled away that morning. Toad was suddenly very angry. "It's not fair, it's just not fair," he grumbled.

The hammering suddenly stopped and Toad opened his eyes, startled by the silence. Clouds hung low in the sky playing keep-away with the last rays of yellow sunlight, and thunder rumbled in the mountains.

And then he heard it—a slipping, sliding sound, the sound of a thousand hissing snakes. Zlotnick was coming with the sled to get the stove! And it wasn't even Saturday yet. Poised at the opening of his burrow, he was getting ready to dash for safety, when down the lane from the shed came the strangest sight Toad had ever seen.

First came Zlotnick, pulling the wooden sled that he used to move heavy pieces of junk. Behind the sled, pushing it, were Crystal and Frieda and Pearlie and Huey. And riding on the sled, with Melba inside it, was a brand-new, bright blue doghouse.

The roof was shingled with new cedar shingles, and there was a swinging door to keep out the rain and a front porch to lie on when the days were warm. There was even a window with a real pane of glass in it and two white shutters on either side.

Toad gasped in amazement as the procession passed him, for over the door of the doghouse was painted the name *Max*.

Down the lane they went until they reached the back of the junkyard where the dog was chained.

"Now, you kids keep out of Papa's way, you hear?" Zlotnick said as the new house came to a halt before the startled dog.

Wide-eyed and with ears up, the black dog backed as far away from them as his chain would allow.

"First we get rid of this mess," Zlotnick said as he put the sheet of plywood back on the lumber pile and tossed aside the scrap of cardboard. Next, with a lot of advice from Crystal and Pearlie, he raked the ground until it was smooth and level. Even Melba did her part, polishing

the windowpane with her Papa's bandana until it sparkled. At last they were ready.

With the children pushing and Zlotnick pulling, the magnificent blue doghouse slid off onto the ground. For a long while the six of them fussed over it, making sure the door was facing so the cold winter wind wouldn't blow inside and the window was placed so Maximillian could look out during the day and see what was going on in the junkyard.

"And keep an eye on Huey," Toad thought to himself as he watched the goings-on.

Crystal found some stones, and with Frieda's help carried them to the new doghouse and put them carefully around the front porch. "So he won't track mud up onto his nice new porch," she explained to Huey, who ran to get his own contribution.

Then Zlotnick unchained Maximillian and murmured, "Good old Max, good old boy." He scratched him behind the ears for what seemed to Toad a very long time. Then he snapped the dog's chain to a shiny brass ring on the side of the new doghouse.

"Now, *that's* a proper home for our junkyard dog," Zlotnick said as he stood back to admire their work.

Pearlie laughed and clapped her hands. "Mean old Slobber."

"Max," Frieda said sternly.

"Nice doggie," Huey crowed.

"No," Crystal said, shaking her head. "He's not a nice doggie, he's a junkyard dog. Junkyard dogs aren't supposed to be nice doggies."

"That's right. But he's the best doggone dog a man could have, and he'll always have a home in my junkyard," Zlotnick said, hitching up his overalls. "He better not get too lazy, though. I'm not sure I can afford *two* junkyard dogs."

THAT NIGHT, after Zlotnick had taken his children home, Toad could hardly wait to make his way through the pelting rain to the new doghouse and inspect it.

In the course of his midnight rounds, Maximillian found Toad beside the porch, trying to peer inside the house.

"It's magnificent! A house to be proud of!" Max declared, shaking the rain out of his rough coat. "And the carpet is blue."

"Congratulations," Toad said. "Zlotnick has finally found himself the perfect dog."

Toad sighed. "Well, I must be going. The ground is wet and I can dig a new burrow now. Tomorrow is Saturday and they're coming to take away my stove."

"Have you decided where you will go?" the dog asked, padding along behind him.

"Someplace safe, someplace permanent. I hate having to move," Toad told him. "I like living in Zlotnick's junkyard but nothing here seems to last very long." Feeling miserable, Toad crawled away, still searching hopefully among the piles of junk.

"I know a place where you can dig your burrow and no one will ever bother you again," the dog said, catching up with Toad by the old bathtub.

"Nowhere," Toad answered. "Nothing is permanent in Zlotnick's junkyard."

"Some things are," the dog said with a grin that showed all of his nice sharp teeth.

Toad stopped crawling and stared at the ugly black dog. Of course. Why hadn't he thought of it?

And so that night, while the rain fell about him, Toad dug a new burrow under the bright blue doghouse. He even added a fancy right-hand turn at the back, although he knew no one would ever dare to investigate a small black hole beneath the house of a mean junkyard dog.

And from that time on, Max spent his days sleeping on the soft carpet of his new doghouse, while Toad was below in his burrow waiting for night to fall.

And every night the two friends hunted together, Toad for the wily old cockroaches and shiny black beetles that

lived among the junk, and Maximillian for the thieves
that threatened to rob Zlotnick's junkyard. Toad was a
fierce hunter and Max was a mean junkyard dog.